Loving Oneness

by
Barry Thomas Bechta

UNCONDITIONAL
LOVE BOOKS

*Redefining, Guiding, and Inspiring Humanity's
Connection to the Creative Power within.*

Loving Oneness
by
Barry Thomas Bechta

Library and Archives Canada Cataloguing in Publication

Bechta, Barry Thomas, 1968-
    Loving oneness / Barry Thomas Bechta.

ISBN 978-0-9813485-0-6

    I. Title.

PS8603.E417L69 2009   C813'.6   C2009-906529-0

Loving Oneness

This book is lovingly dedicated to
Kimiko Nicole von Boetticher

red

rain

The rain darkened the midnight sky and limited Martin's vision as it cascaded down the windshield of his car in one solid sheet. The wiper blades did very little to clear the waterfall away. The streetlights refracted through the water and blinded Martin every few seconds. He could not see clearly, even so, he still drove too fast.

Martin fiddled with the car radio and switched from station to station searching for an adrenaline rushing song. He could not find one so he began pulling CDs from the glove compartment. He read their titles and placed the older CDs on the seat beside him. When Martin finally saw the perfect CD, he strained to grasp it, but the seat belt held him in place so he pulled it off his shoulder to reach farther.

Through his peripheral vision, Martin first saw the red traffic light mutating in the rain waterfall. He sat up and strained to look out the obscured windshield, but he could not see anything clearly. He hoped there were no cars in the intersection. His eyes followed inches behind the wiper blades. They searched for a clear pathway. They only saw a man.

Time stopped!

The man's face was ghostly white in the bright headlights.

Martin slammed on the brakes. The loud music playing on the radio, and the thundering rain on the car body covered the sound of impact. The man's body drifted away from the car and fell down out of Martin's sight. The car inched forward a few more feet before it stopped its agonizing skid and time returned to normal.

Martin shifted the gear into park, jumped out of the car, and ran up to the motionless body. He watched the rain explode in a red pool of blood around the man's head. Martin panicked and ran back to the car. He backed the car away from the body and turned around in the middle of the street. He sped away and time stood still a second time.

A radiant light gleamed into Martin's eyes through the rearview mirror. The light mesmerized him. In the heart of the light a woman emerged. She knelt beside the fallen man and placed a hand on his forehead. The man sat up and then a brilliant flash blinded Martin.

As quickly as the light had arrived, it left, and the two figures disappeared with it. At the next street corner, Martin turned the car right and his memory of the accident vanished immediately as his car rounded the corner.

orange

dream

The dream was too real to be a dream. In the dream, Chris left his Friday night youth group dance to walk home in a deafening downpour. It was raining so hard that Chris could barely see a few feet in front of him. Chris stopped at a corner and waited for the light to change. When it did he stepped into the intersection and the droplets of rain glowed around him. He turned to his left and saw a pair of headlights. They pushed him backwards through the air. He landed flat on his back and the breath vanished from his lungs. His head sounded a dull thud and did not bounce.

The stars above Chris looked peaceful. His spirit flew towards them. It soared and spun in an unrestricted and blissful flight. On his forth revolution, he noticed his body lying on the ground and the forceful rain washing the blood away from under the body's head. The lifeless quality of his body did not affect him so he turned away from it and flew in the direction of the stars once more in the crystal clear sky.

The stars rotated clockwise, slow at first as their light stretched and trailed across each other forming the walls of an ebony tunnel with a solitary light at the tunnel's distant centre. The light's gentle radiance was warm; not in temperature, but in a feeling of love. A love so encompassing and inviting, it was all Chris was conscious about.

"It's not time." a Voiceless Voice said and Chris' spirit jumped back into his body of brilliant light.

In his bedroom, Chris sat up and gasped for air. With his eyes closed, he could still sense the dream; it was loving and kind, but fading.

beach

The sun rose silently and greeted a woman meditating on the beach. It illuminated the woman and a man that silently watched her from a distance. When the sun was free of the horizon, the woman nodded in gratitude to the sun, stood up, and proceeded down the beach. The man walked up to her and struck up a conversation. Even though they had never met, the woman knew everything about the man as if she had know him since the beginning of time. The man found the woman's awareness of his life comforting.

By noon, forty people sat on logs and in the sand around the woman and listened as she spoke.

"We create our reality." the woman said, "Nothing occurs by chance. The power to destroy or create our own dreams lies within us."

"You mean, there are no victims." A man said from the crowd.

"There are victims for those who choose to be. But only we can choose for ourselves to experience something."

"What about when other people do things to me?" another woman asked.

"No one ever does anything to us, unless we choose it. A choice can be made consciously or unconsciously. Either way, we ask for everything we experience by our choice, or our lack of choice."

"There is no way I chose my life to be as it is." Someone spoke out.

"You choose your thoughts about your world. No one else can choose your thoughts for you. And people show up to match your thoughts about the world."

"I didn't ask my brother to steal my wife." One man said.

"I didn't ask my neighbour to treat me like garbage." Another man added.

"I most certainly didn't ask my coworker to lie and take credit for my work." a woman said.

The woman leading the discussion continued, "We create our beliefs through the stories we tell. Every story we tell attracts to us whatever we think about. We can think about abundance, or lack, about working more, or allowing abundance to flow to us passively. Each and every thought we use directs energy into whatever we think. Ask and it shall be given, means absolutely everything we think about, both the things we want and the things we don't want.

"We could say something off-the-cuff like, 'the summer heat makes people lazy.' And this simple unconscious belief seems to be about no one in particular, yet we have used a broad brush stroke to paint everyone with one belief, without even being aware we have done so. Now our brother can show up as lazy to prove this unconscious belief, or our neighbour, or our coworker.

"We may consciously choose to believe that our brother lies, cheats, or steals, and we discover that our brother lies, cheats, or steals to prove our beliefs are correct.

"Another person may consciously choose to believe that our brother is honest, helpful, and generous, and our brother shows up for them as honest, helpful, and generous to prove their beliefs are correct."

"And yes, life even has the ability to orchestrate circumstances and events to prove both person's beliefs are right simultaneously."

Someone asked, "So what can we do to control our thoughts?"

"Tell good feeling stories about your life as you want to experience it. Consciously choose your beliefs about the things you wish to see in life. If you wish more love, choose good feeling thoughts about love. If you wish more abundance, choose good feeling thoughts about abundance. Anything you wish to experience more of, choose good feeling thoughts about it and you will experience it."

A four year old girl with blond hair in pigtails and a smile to melt any heart walked up to the woman. The girl held an orange in her hands, which she presented to the woman. The woman sat down on a log so she would be near the height of the girl.

"What's your name?" The woman asked.

"Judy."

"Thank you for your gift, Judy."

The woman placed the orange into an empty basket she pulled from thin air behind the log she sat upon. Then she covered the basket with a towel, which she also pulled, just as effortlessly, from the air behind the log. Next the woman leaned over and whispered into Judy's ear. Judy nodded in agreement and walked to the closest person.

"Would you like to have an orange?" Judy asked.

"Please."

The woman carried the towel covered basket and followed Judy from person to person. Everyone smiled as they moved through the crowd and Judy reached under the towel covered basket and presented orange after orange. A wave of exhilaration washed through the crowd as each new orange appeared from within the basket.

park

Martin lay on the uncut grass in the park. He inhaled the thick scent of summer wafting past his nose on this sunny afternoon. The fragrance enlivened his spirits, but something made him feel uneasy. He could not figure out what was bothering him, so he decided to burn away his worries in the sun. He closed his eyes and created a peaceful space in his mind. He listened to the sounds of birds and was almost asleep when an intense light focussed on his face. He blocked the light with an outstretched hand and squinted his eyes to look at the source. The light was brilliant and he could not make out anything as images flooded his mind: a car, a man, a pool of blood, a light, and a woman.

When the light shifted, the images in Martin's mind faded and he noticed a group of people walking down the hill in front of him following a woman. Martin felt pulled in their direction. He stood up and walked towards the group and he began to hear the woman's words as he got closer.

"Do what you really love. There are no mistakes." she said.

A man disagreed, "Mistakes happen all the time."

"Everything works out in the end. When you look back on your life as a whole, you shall see the perfection of it all. So do what you really love. Have more fun."

"That sounds selfish." a woman in the crowd said.

"To do as you really love is practical and loving and completely self fulfilling. When you do what you love, your sense of love grows and you have more love to give to others. When you love yourself, you feel good and share good with everyone. No one who truly loves themselves harms another."

Martin listened and moved to the front of the group.

The woman pulled two more oranges from the towel covered basket. These oranges were the size of grapefruits. The woman held the orange in her right hand up for everyone to see. and the woman said, "We are like oranges. When we squeeze an orange we get orange juice. When we let another person squeeze us, by their actions, we let out whatever is within us." As she squeezed the orange and its fresh liquid ran through her fingers and down her arm she said, "For some of us it will be the orange juice of love."

The woman next raised her left hand and squeezed the second orange. Orange juice flowed forth as she squeezed it and then she said. "For others it will be the orange juice of hate." And as she squeezed the orange further a solid blackness the consistency of oil came forth. "We can only give to the world whatever we choose to marinate in."

The woman next placed both hands together saying, "I choose only Love." And the oily blackness that coated her left arm refreshed to its pure sparkling orange clarity.

Hours later, when the woman finished speaking, the setting sun glowed orange against the clouds on the blue-green sky. She thanked everyone for the love they had experienced together. Then the woman walked around the tree she had leaned against during the last hour, and disappeared when she did. The crowd walked off into the night talking about miracles to each other. Martin knew in his heart that he would meet this woman again.

yellow

park bench

The tall pines of the park were surrounded by schools of dandelions. The full yellow blooms opened wide in the afternoon sun as they yielded to the radiant light.

The woman sat on a park bench in the shade. The crowd of people that had followed her the day before were not around. Martin approached her and stopped in front of the woman. She smiled at Martin.

"Am I evil?" he asked.

"Judge nothing and then ask your question." she said.

Martin thought about the woman's response. "Judge nothing? Am I evil? I am someone. Is there anyone that is evil? Anyone is someone. Judge nothing! Is there anything that is evil?"

"Whether something is good or evil is based on your beliefs about that very thing."

"Is there more evil today than a couple hundred years ago?"

"No."

"More war?"

"No."

"Abuse?"

"No."

"More violence?" He asked.

"No."

"How can your answer always be, 'No' when there appears to be a lot of it today."

"All of life is made of appearances. The things you choose to believe colour the things that appear in your life. You give all the meaning to your life by what you choose to believe. So let me ask you a different question. Is there more *love* today than a couple hundred years ago?"

"I'm not sure." he said, "Is there?"

"No."

"I don't understand."

"The universe is composed entirely of energy. That energy manifests in different forms, yet the amount of energy in the cosmos is constant; constantly changing and constantly staying the same. Energy cannot be created from nothing and it cannot be destroyed. Love and Violence are the same energy in different forms."

"Love and violence are the same thing?"

"Love and violence are composed of the same energy, they are definitely not the same thing. Everything is composed of God Life Energy." The woman smiled again, though she had never really stopped smiling, and then added, "You could say that the bad of life is God's Love cleverly disguised . . . Martin."

At the moment the woman said Martin's name, he felt total peace. He did not know this woman, yet he knew that she knew everything about him. The woman's smile went directly into Martin and he opened his carefully guarded heart to her presence and the questions that had troubled him seconds earlier; questions that had troubled him for years; questions that he could never answer disappeared. It was not that he had forgotten them. Martin realized that the energy of life made love and violence and the sun and the woman and him and in that instant all of his questions were answered or appeared unimportant which amounted to the same thing.

Then in the next instant Martin asked, "Did I do something wrong the other night?"

"I thought you were going to make it this time."

"This time?"

"You are going to make it, Martin." she promised him and held out her hand, "By the way, my name is Nicole."

He shook her hand, "I'm . . . well you know who I am."

"Yes."

"It's very nice to meet you, Nicole. Do you live near here?"

Nicole laughed out loud.

"You could say, I'm just visiting."

"Friends?" Martin asked.

"Yes, friends." She laughed again. "About what happened the other night, judge nothing and ask your question."

The accident flooded Martin's mind once more; the car, the rain, the man, the blood. He tried to think of his actions as energy. He tried to tell himself that energy is always present; love and violence and happiness and sadness and the car and the man; but the blood, the blood was wrong. Energy or not, he knew it was wrong. He knew he was judging himself, but he had to. If he did not judge himself, who would?

As a boy, Martin had believed in a God that judged, but over the years he convinced himself that their was no such thing as a judging God. Martin decided that whatever he could not see, could not be. Two nights ago, he saw something that was miraculous. Remembering this, Martin felt totally connected with all of life and totally separate from it all and this felt lonely.

"When you judge nothing about yourself you know you are loved, no matter what." Nicole said.

Inside Martin's chest, a crushing grip released its grasp. Nicole smiled at Martin and he felt relief.

"Is there really a God?" he asked.

"Would it matter if there really were a God, or not?"

"I think so."

"Why?"

"Because . . . well I . . . I hate God." Martin said. "I hate God because He either doesn't exist, or if He does exist, He doesn't really care about humanity. Have you seen the world today? It's a mess."

"I promise you it's a message to help you feel better, and 'no' I do not see the world as you do because I have different thoughts about this world. I cannot make you believe my beliefs as I do. I can share my beliefs with you. In order for you to believe something you have to experience it first hand. Then you will choose to confirm your beliefs by what already fits with your world view. I cannot choose something for you, and you cannot choose something for me or anyone else. You always have choice."

"You mean free will, right?"

"Yes. God cares so much for this world that He gives us free will over our thoughts. On earth we can choose to believe in our connection to the Divine, or we can choose to believe in our separation from the Divine. God's greatest gift to humanity is the ability to choose to believe in God or not. Angels don't even have the privilege of free will."

"Really?"

"Really."

"Are you an angel?" Martin asked.

"Heavens no. I like free will too much. God actually approves of all lives and all ways of life through free will."

"Seriously?"

"God creates only perfection. God gives only perfection. God sees only perfection. God is only perfection."

"That sounds like a load of pollyanna to me."

"How do you feel when you say that?"

"I felt good making a joke."

"Did you really? Or were you ignoring your true feelings through a joke?"

"Maybe."

"Choose to feel joyful." Nicole said. "Joy connects you with Source. Become aware of your true feelings and let everything else go. Forget about all your worries and fears and concerns."

"Forget about them. Don't I have to correct my past actions?"

"You can't change the past. You can only make what you do in this moment the best you possibly can. Beating yourself up about something from your past keeps you feeling bad in this moment. Let your bad thoughts about your past go. If you can't choose any good thoughts about it, think about something else totally."

"Is that responsible?"

"When you insist that you're sinful, evil, or imperfect because of something in your past, you use God Life Energy in this moment to attract more experiences like that for yourself. The present moment is your access point to everything that manifests in your life. Whatever you place your attention onto, you also place your energy into. Let your pain go to let your joy grow. Just one single thought that moves you towards feeling a little better is the way back to joy and if life ever seems too tough, let go of your painful burdens, and let God take care of them for you."

skytrain

The yellow sun blazed through the window of the skytrain. Martin and Nicole sat beside each other. The sun's radiance disappeared and reappeared behind the wire and steel of the bridge as the skytrain travelled across the afternoon sky.

"So I ask you, Martin, 'do you still hate God?'"

"Maybe hate is too strong a word."

"Does that thought feel better?"

"Yes that thought feels good."

"God feels good."

The train pulled into the next station and slowed to a stop. Chris's tall thin form walked out of the train car and stepped onto the platform. The dream he had had the morning before rose to the surface of his mind. He saw the headlights rushing towards him; he saw the driver of the car. Chris now realized that Martin was the driver of that car in his dream.

As the train pulled from the station, Chris turned around to look at Martin. He did not know Martin. He did not even know his name, but a ball of anger formed in his stomach upon seeing this man from his dream. Chris silently condemned both Martin and Nicole because they were together.

Chris tried to calm the anger building within, but it raged.

He remembered their conversation on the train. *What a couple of religious freaks*, he thought.

"God!" he exploded loud enough that most everyone on the platform turned to look. Then Chris walked across the platform and down the stairs and over to the bus stop.

"Religions freaks suck!" he yelled at the top of his lungs.

All of the people at the bus stop kept their distance from Chris without making it look like they were keeping their distance.

green

basketball court

Martin and Nicole rode the skytrain to the end of the line. They disembarked and walked from the station to a nearby park where they sat on the midsummer green grass. A group of youth played basketball on a court behind them. Nicole spoke to Martin.

"The *miracle* is your reaction to the accident."

"But something impossible, is that not a miracle?"

"So how do you explain what happened?"

"It was a miracle."

"Which is something that's impossible?"

"Something that's impossible for me." Martin said.

"Only you?"

"Most people."

"Everyone creates miracles every day."

"So, how do you create a miracle?"

"You choose one conscious unchanging thought about something in order to experience it." Nicole said, "You just become one with that which you wish to see."

"How long does it take?"

"When chosen completely it is . . . "

apartment at dusk

" . . . instantaneous."

Nicole held one conscious unchanging thought with her entire being, and they instantly materialized in Martin's apartment.

Martin looked around stunned.

"The universe is energy." Nicole said while Martin absorbed the transformation, "And a miracle is one way we can direct God Life Energy."

"So I could make a miracle happen?"

"All of life is a miracle happening. We choose what we wish to be until we finally see it. It usually takes so long because we keep changing our minds about what we want to see, and the results that appear keep changing until we get wherever we are going."

"Can you guide me through this miracle process?"

"First, think of something simple, a small simple miracle."

Martin thought of lighting the candle that sat on the table between the two of them.

"Okay." he said.

"Now, imagine energy in the form of a white light as bright as the sun. Imagine being one with that light. Feel it filling your entire being and energizing every cell in your body." she said, "Take individual particles of this light energy and build an image of your chosen miracle and when you feel really joyous or total peace, you can relax knowing your miracle is complete."

Martin closed his eyes while Nicole directed him through the miracle process. He felt at one with the white light that filled his being. The light coursed through his body and he felt alive. In his mind's eye, he constructed a flickering candle flame and watched it burn blissfully. Then a sense of peace washed over his body. He opened his eyes and looked at the candle.

"It didn't work." He said.

"What did you want to do?"

"I wanted to light this candle." Martin said pointing his index finger towards it. A yellow flame burned effortlessly from his fingertip.

"Oh I forgot to mention one thing." Nicole said. "You have to place your miracle in a specific context. In this case, the candle flame with the actual candle."

Martin lit the candle with his finger tip and then blew out the flame. "Wow I did it, but will it be that easy when you're not here?"

"I may have guided you through the process, but you did it Martin."

"So, I'll be able to do this again?"

"When you choose one conscious unchanging good feeling thought about anything, you eventually experience it. Most people only ask for miracles when they are feeling desperate. The only time we can create a miracle occurs when we are feeling definite about our connection with God Life Energy."

"Feeling definite, not desperate. Got it!"

"Forget about this type of physical miracle and focus on the most effective miracle everyone has access to."

"Which is?"

"The direction of your thought to feel better. When you tell a story that feels good to you, you will feel better. The better you feel, the better feeling your life experience becomes. That is the greatest miracle of all."

apartment at night

Nicole walked out onto the balcony and looked up at the moon and stars. Martin joined her and they sat down on the balcony and Nicole said, "Most people don't realize we create all of our experiences by what we think. We see the results of our simple unchanging good feeling thoughts; make a dinner, take a walk, compliment someone. However, we rarely see that the complex situations in our lives are the results of a whole bunch of simple habitual bad feeling thoughts mixed together. It is our bad feeling thoughts that create havoc in our future."

"But, I can't see the future." Martin said.

"Most of us can't see the exact time, place, people, or way our actions will materialize in the future, but we all can always feel the energy of our thoughts and understand how that energy is going to come back feeling to us."

"Can we control that energy?"

"We cannot control energy that we have already used, but we can use all new energy in a controlled manner."

"So we should try to use energy in a positive way?"

"When we use energy in *a positive way* for us, the energy goes out into the universe and affects everyone differently. Some will be affected positively and others will be affected negatively because of their thoughts. There is no universally positive way to do anything that all people will agree upon."

apartment at dawn

"All of God Life Energy moves in a circular motion."

Nicole raised her hand into the air and moved it in a clockwise motion as she continued.

Life

Experiences **Thoughts**

Things **Feelings**

Places **Words**

People **Actions**

Love

23

"God Life Energy forms All That Is; All people, places, things, and experiences. Life is at the top, because life is all there is. From the human perspective there appears to be the limit of our physical forms, but there is no real death. Physical forms can die. Our spirit is eternally alive. The seasons show us the eternal nature of the life cycle.

"You know the saying, 'What goes around comes around'. That is this circle. The energy we use in life through our thoughts, feelings, words, and actions sets up our energy frequency that attract people, places, things, and experiences of matching energy on the cycle of life.

"Lower frequency experiences are ruled by our bad feeling emotions. Lower frequencies never consume us. We live with them when we experience pain, suffering, anxiety, worry, and fear which by their very frequencies can only attract more of the same feeling experiences into our lives.

"All experiences give us the opportunity to choose what we believe about life. Only when our energy frequency is infused with confidence, joy, and pleasure do we attract more of the same into our lives. All experiences, no matter what they may be, are there for us to move towards more Love in the cycle. Our higher frequency experiences are ruled by our good feeling emotions.

"Our energy use attracts matching energy experiences. We really do create everything in our life. Love attracts love. Hate attracts hate. Pain attracts pain. Joy attracts joy. Our personal energy is made of our beliefs, our memories, and our habits in action.

"Now I ask you, Martin, 'what happens to a person's energy when they die?'"

"When a person dies . . . since their energy is not destroyed, the transformed energy would be at the same rate of vibration in its new form. Since we take our beliefs and memories and habits with us we are basically the same being in spirit as we were in the flesh."

"We are similar, but not the same. When we die we release all limiting beliefs we ever held. In spirit there is no pain. In spirit manifestation is instantaneous. In spirit we are limitless."

"Why would we ever become human then?"

"For the fun."

"This is fun?"

"Oh yeah. In spirit there is no drama. In spirit anything we could ever desire manifests instantly. Actually it's even faster than instantaneous because every potential is present at the same time, kind of multi-taneous.

"On earth there is a lag time. On earth we have to hold a thought with feeling consistently for manifestation to occur. Sometimes we do it with bad feelings and sometimes with good feelings."

"All for fun?"

"We choose to believe in disconnection from Source over and over again until we see and choose our one conscious unchanging good feeling thought about our eternal connection with God Life Energy. Because the experience of it all is glorious."

"But why would we choose to believe in disconnection?"

"Earth is the ultimate spa retreat away from God. Earth is the Ultimate free will Experience. Free will allows us to fight life. Free will allows us to deny life. Free will allows us to Ultimately

Benefit life. There is real perfection in the design."

blue

downtown

Puffy white clouds floated effortlessly across the blue sky. Chris did not notice them though. He was happy the sun was out and that it was warm, but he did not look into the sky. The white clouds passed in front of Chris and their reflections passed behind him on the mirrored windows of the tall skyscraper he waited beside. Occasionally, the clouds blocked the sun and Chris felt cooler, but they quickly moved across the sky and the sun warmed him once again.

Chris' mind was wrapped up in the work day ahead of him. He could not think very clearly, however, because the diesel smell of the idling buses fuelled his headache.

Nicole walked passed Chris and stopped a few feet away. Nicole's presence infuriated Chris. He looked away and tried to let his feelings pass. This worked until a man approached Nicole.

"If no one has told you today," she said, "God loves you."

"You don't know the first thing about God!" Chris yelled over to them.

Nicole looked at Chris calmly and then returned to her conversation with the man.

"Leave him alone lady! Do you like being preached to?"

The man with Nicole felt uncomfortable for her and gently grabbed her elbow and said, "Let's move down this way."

They moved up the street and out of Chris's sight. Even with them gone, he bitched and complained to the people around him until his bus arrived.

lake

Martin and Nicole sat by the edge of an azure lake. Martin threw a pebble into the still water, marring its mirrored surface.

"The lake is like the universe." Nicole said, "That small pebble is you. The waves are your energy use. When you do anything in the universe, the energy from your actions spread out into the universe."

Martin nodded.

"Imagine that this large rock is a catastrophic event, like the death of a loved one."

Nicole thrust the rock into the lake. It made a magnificent splash and large waves moved out from the impact point.

"How does the energy affect you?" Nicole asked.

"Its large energy waves take over my smaller energy waves."

"Do they?"

Martin looked at the waves on the water and thought about it. "No. They only appear more powerful than my smaller waves."

"How does the energy affect you then?"

"The large energy waves of the death make my smaller waves of everyday life appear less noticeable."

"What do your smaller waves represent?"

"They represent me."

"The pebble is you."

"That's right. The waves are my energy in the world."

"So how does the death affect you then?"

"It only affects me if I let the energy take me on the roller coaster ride of emotions."

"Can you stop it from doing that?"

"Detachment." Martin said.

"Detachment is the principle, but how does it work in practice?"

"If the large rock is the death of a loved one, the death affects me when I take the energy on. However, if I think of all the people who die each day around the world, I realize that most don't affect me because I am detached from them."

"Why do we create these experiences for ourselves?"

"Well . . . " Martin started, "we choose to believe we are

separate from others and God, so we can choose to feel connection with others and God."

Nicole smiled and let that thought sink in.

"Can we experience no grief when a loved one dies?" Nicole asked.

"I imagine we can through detachment, but I don't see how."

"It's a feeling thing. When you have the thought that your loved one is dead and you feel separate and sad, you are attached to your bad feeling thoughts and believing they are true. When you have the thought that your loved one is dead and you feel connected and joyful knowing that there is eternal life, you are attached to the Divine's thought about your eternal loved one. This good feeling supports your connection with your departed loved one too."

dusk

The sky turned shades of blue-green after the sun had set. Martin and Nicole started to walk around the lake in the twilight. The trees crackled with energy as they cooled down from the summer heat. Bats darted in crooked lines across the sky catching bugs. Their ballet was silhouetted against the lasts rays of light on the western horizon. The stars sparkled in the black sky to the east.

As they walked in silence, Martin thought of all the things they had talked about during the past few days. He felt like he had been smiled upon and he wondered why. A week ago he had hit a man with his car. Now he was being apprenticed by Nicole. He understood that life was energy, energy circling in the universe, but he wondered how this energy might come back.

"Nicole," Martin asked, "I understand that things happen so we can experience energy, but I wonder if you could help me to better understand how energy works."

"Of course. Think about every situation as a cleverly disguised gift of love. What's the gift in this experience you are having with me?"

"Lots of love! You've given me so much information about life, energy, and everything."

"No, I didn't give you this information."

"I didn't know this stuff."

"From the human perspective, you didn't remember this stuff. From the spiritual perspective you know everything you need to know and can call upon it when you feel connected to all of life. We are all masters in disguise. The more we remember, the more we become active masters. I am sharing some ideas with you, but you are giving yourself this information by accepting it. If I had told a person that didn't want to hear this information, it wouldn't have been heard."

"I can understand that."

"Talking about some things are an easy way to remember for some people and harder for others. You are open to these gifts of love. Sometimes our gifts of love come cleverly disguised in challenging forms."

"So, I should be able to see the reason for the accident?"

"Be able to, yes. Should, No. You're caught up in the emotions of that experience. The more emotionally affected you become, the greater the gift of love available to you. When you talk about 'the accident', you only see that experience from a physical perspective. When you talk about 'the cleverly disguised gift of love', you are beginning to see it from a spiritual perspective."

Martin picked up a pebble and threw it into the lake. The stars stretched and danced in the rings moving out from the pebble's impact point.

"So, I planned for this experience to happen." Martin said.

"Yes, but not consciously. Why would you have unconsciously planned an experience like this?"

"For the fun."

"Be more specific."

"Maybe we *both* had to learn about love, but from different points of view."

"Which was positive and which was negative?"

Martin said, "Something is positive or negative depending on perspective only."

"Now you're remembering this stuff. What is love?" Nicole asked.

"Love is . . . fun."

"You bet love is fun. People come together to share their cleverly wrapped gifts of love to have fun together. You both came together because you have a gift of love to share with each other. And you love the drama of it all."

"I find this fun?" Martin wondered.

"Totally."

"And to have fun, all I need to do is the things I love?"

"Try to do the things you hate and see how quickly that takes you to misery. Do the things you love and see how quickly that takes you to ecstasy. How anyone takes what you do in life is their business. Focus on what you love and what brings you joy and your energy frequency will attract people, places, things, and experiences of the same joyous energy vibration. I am one of those new friends that has come into your life. In fact, all three of us planned this experience together."

"Are you talking with the guy I hit the other night?"

"I am spending time with him."

"Are you in two places at once? "

"Not right now. Even so, he and I are learning something totally different together."

"You actually know him."

"I know him and I remember that I know him. He doesn't remember me though. You don't remember him either. And for the record, the three of us are best friends in spirit. Everyone in our life shows us what we really believe about ourselves at the deepest levels and about God Life Energy at the highest levels."

Martin said, "So every person, place, thing, and experience in our life is a cleverly wrapped gift of love."

"Precisely."

"But isn't that too simple?"

"Life is simple. If it were too easy, we'd never experience any drama or fun, would we?"

indigo

bird

A few days had passed since Martin and Nicole's last visit. Martin sat in his living room eating a peanut butter sandwich while unsuccessfully trying to light a candle with energy. The image Martin constructed in his mind disappeared when a thud at the patio door startled him. He got up to see what had hit the door. A bird fluttered frantically on the balcony for a few seconds, but it could not lift its head from the balcony floor. Suddenly, the flurry of wings stopped and the bird lay on its belly in a daze. Its chest extended and contracted deeply with each breath. The top of the bird's head was bright indigo.

"Are you going to be alright little one?" Martin asked.

The bird closed its eyes and continued breathing heavily. It seemed to be calm and panicked at the same time. Martin watched the bird breathe and he thought of helping the bird, but he was not sure how. When an idea flashed in his mind, Martin walked quickly to the kitchen and filled a soup bowl with water. The whiteness of the bowl made him think of white light and he filled his body with it and visualized a healthy bird flying into the blue sky. Martin then grabbed a bird identification book from his book shelf, but when he returned to the living room, the bird was gone. He looked the bird up in his bird identification book and read its name.

"Indigo Bunting: a North American finch. The male's head

and upper parts are bright indigo."

children

The next day after Martin had finished work he got in his car to drive home. It was the first time he had driven past the intersection since the accident and the memory flooded his mind.

A girl screamed and Martin rushed back to the reality of driving and slammed on the breaks to will his car to a stop. In his daydream, he had almost hit a group of children crossing the street in broad daylight. He was not exceptionally close, but he had definitely been unaware. If it had not been for the girl's scream, he most certainly would have hit one or more of the children. He breathed a deep sigh of relief.

television

At home, Martin turned on the television and flipped through the channels until a show about Buddhism caught his attention. He watched and listened to the narrator.

"In Buddhism, Karma results from an individual's actions in life. The actions in one lifetime influence the tests for consecutive lifetimes. The individual attains release from Karma and the cycle of reincarnation when the individual has balanced all karmic debts. This balancing of debts allows the individual to move to the state of Nirvana." The narrator continued, "Nirvana is the beatific spiritual condition attained through the extinction of desire."

That is like energy, Martin thought. We have to be detached from our emotions to consciously control energy.

●●●

Across town, Chris watched the same program on his television. It made some sense to him. He had thought of reincarnation and karma, but he did not really believe in it. He had not dismissed it though. He felt more comfortable with the single life and afterlife concept, even though that belief left a lot to be desired. He could not believe in a God that let so much pain and suffering be present in the world.

mountain

At five-thirty, Martin felt energized. He decided to hike up a local mountain to watch the sunset. He checked the forecast on the Weather Network; it said hot and sunny. He changed into shorts and put his hiking boots into the car and then drove the half hour to the base of the small mountain.

The sun was still hot and the sky cloudless when he started his hike at six o'clock. For the first half hour Martin hiked under tree cover, but the next half hour was spotted with sunshine. He drank from a water bottle when he needed liquids and he reached the top of the mountain two hours before sunset. Martin sat in the grass facing the warm sun.

"Karma!" he yelled off the top of the mountain.

He waited for an echo even though he knew there wouldn't be one.

"Not Karma." an echo whispered.

Martin laughed nervously. He turned his head to look

around. No one was there and he felt a chill run up his spine and the hair rise on the back of his neck. There was no doubt about it. He had heard the voice.

"Something funny?" the echo asked as a hand grabbed his shoulder.

"What the hell!" Martin screamed at the top of his lungs and jumped and ran a dozen steps before turning around.

"Are you alright?" Nicole laughed.

"Yeah." Martin said, "Well no." His heart pounded in his chest, "You scared the heck out of me."

"You scared the heck out of *yourself*."

"Yeah I guess I did." he said and laughed with Nicole.

"What are you afraid of?"

"The unknown, I guess."

"What's unknown?"

"The voice! I thought it was God or I was crazy or . . . "

"Or?"

"I don't know."

"What don't you know?"

"Lots!"

"What is the universe made of?"

"Energy."

"What's not to know then?"

"Lots!" Martin said.

"What is the universe made of?" Nicole asked again.

"Energy."

"What's not to know?"

"Did I miss something?"

"I am beginning to think so."

"Me too." Martin said and they laughed together.

"I want to clarify something." Nicole said, "There is no karma."

"It seems to explain a lot of bad things in life."

"Life is actually much simpler than karma."

"How so?"

"It's your thoughts that create your life."

"I've heard this before, but it seems inconsistent."

"That because it's only consistent for each person. Here's

the way it works. Thought. Feeling. Experience. A *good* thought for your individual perspective feels *good* to you and you alone. Your *good* feeling thoughts will eventually manifest as *good* feeling experiences for you and you alone."

"What about bad feeling thoughts?"

"A *bad* thought for your individual perspective feels *bad* to you and you alone. Your *bad* feeling thoughts will eventually manifest as *bad* feeling experiences for you and you alone."

"For me and me alone?"

"Others may agree with your good or bad feeling thoughts about your experience some of the time on some things, but at no time could someone find complete agreement with another about every issue to ever come up."

"That sounds bad?"

"No. This is very good. All you have to remember is good thoughts for you feel good to you and lead to good feeling experiences for you."

"That seems very selfish."

"Everyone lives life through a perspective of self. Anyone who claims different is doing that through a perspective of self."

●●●

In silence they watched the sunset after nine-thirty. Martin truly experienced the power of the sun for the first time. He had felt its warmth many times before, but right then he understood its true power. A power that gave life and energy to an entire planet without asking for anything in return. It was beyond incredible. Martin thought about this as the sun disappeared below the horizon.

"We have a long way to walk." Martin said, "We should get started."

"Yes, you should."

"Me?" He said and looked at Nicole, but she had vanished.

"Great."

"You can do this as well." her voice reminded him.

"How?"

"'How?' is all he can say."

Martin tried until he was fed up with trying. Then he walked down the mountain in total darkness. Half way down the mountain, Martin heard Nicole's voice.

"Choose to be, instead of wishing, trying, or desperately wanting to be."

When Martin got to his car he resolved to be happy because he controlled his own happiness by the direction of his thought. He consciously directed his thought to good feeling ideas while he drove home, arriving there around midnight.

violet

bed

"Get up."

"What." Martin woke.

"Today's an important day."

"Why . . . " Martin rubbed his eyes and focussed on Nicole until her image became clear. " . . . are you here?"

"Today you are going to show yourself what you know."

"Leave me alone." Martin rolled over. "I'm sleeping."

"Why do you think you are learning all of this."

Martin threw a pillow at Nicole, "To become a better person."

"That's true, but is this only about you?"

"No."

"Who then?"

"Everyone?"

"Simple." Nicole said.

"What do you mean by simple?"

"Sharing this knowledge with everyone."

"Everyone?"

"Everyone who asks. Go get showered."

Martin returned enlivened from his warm shower.

"Are you asking me to preach?" Martin wondered.

"Why do you say that?"

"Well you said sharing what I know with everyone. That sounds a lot like preaching to me."

"I said, *everyone that asks*."

"So, if no one asks, nothing happens."

"Right."

"Why did I have to get up so early then?"

"It's sunny!"

"Sunny?"

"Yeah, sunny days are great days to get up early."

"I could've slept in. It's still going to be sunny at noon."

"You can tell the future."

"No, I mean . . ." Martin let out a deep breath and changed his thoughts. "Is there anything I should know to say or not to say?"

"Remember that each person cleverly hides their own answers from themselves."

"Why?"

"You tell me."

"For the drama." Martin said.

"For the absolute fun of it all."

seven

They walked into the park bright and early. Way too early from Martin's perspective. Nicole had told him the park was as good a place as any to answer questions. Martin did not recognize anyone in the park, yet he still felt silly in his thoughts.

"Hey Mister can you pass our soccer ball." A boy called from behind Martin.

"Sure." Martin walked up to the ball and kicked it towards the boy.

"Thanks." The boy said.

"No problem."

Martin walked beside the soccer field and watched the boys and girls on the field passing a bunch of soccer balls back and forth for their warm up.

"That's nice of you." said an elderly woman sitting in a wheelchair. "So many people today don't bother anymore."

"You think so?" Martin sat on the bench next to her.

"People today think about themselves, like my daughter. She brought me here to the park and now she is sitting over there with her new beau."

The woman pointed a finger in the direction of a couple on a bench across the soccer field.

"They think about what is good for themselves first and others second. When I was young it was the other way around. First others and then yourself. It's good to see that some young people have picked up good habits."

Martin nodded, curious as to what possible question he might have to answer.

"If people knew about God there would be no wars and no poverty and no sadness. Do you go to church?"

Martin did not answer.

The woman continued, "What would it matter. Most people today believe in a supreme being of some kind, but fewer go to church. People say they can pray in the street as well as in a church. It's true they can, but do they? I believe you'd find that they don't. They're too worried about what experience they're going to try next; sex, drugs; you name it, they try it. The world is degenerating because people lack a true sense of purpose. Many people today use television to set their moral compass."

The woman looked at Martin as if she expected a reply and then continued.

"It is sad that the most powerful tool of the twentieth century is also the poorest utilized one. Television is used to give us information and entertainment and sometimes it is a connector of great distances and people, but it's primarily used for judgments."

"Judgments?" Martin asked.

"The news, movies, talk shows, television dramas; they all create a forum for us to judge others. Try to deny it."

Martin tried to deny the idea as the woman continued to talk. He could not deny it. Still he wondered if God were everything everywhere, then television would be as much God as he or the woman or anything else would be.

"So what do you say to all of that?" the woman asked.

"I think that you have said a lot of thought provoking ideas."

"You bet I have."

The woman talked for a little while longer and then Martin wished the woman a good day and continued his way across the park to the place Nicole stood.

"I see you met Mary."

"You know her?"

"I know everyone. So do you."

"She didn't ask me any question."

"Her question is the same question most people have."

"What is the question most people have?"

"Do you see my value?"

"She never asked that."

"People want to be heard. There is nothing a person finds more connecting with Source than truly being heard by another. Did you truly listen to Mary's words?"

"I think so."

"Did you listen for the ideas that felt good in what she shared?"

"I tried."

"You can do that with everyone you meet."

"What if they share bad feeling stories."

"You can focus onto good feeling ideas, or excuse yourself when you cannot feel good in a person's presence."

"That sounds selfish again."

"Once again I remind you, we all see life through the very individual perspective of self. Unless you are feeling good in your perspective of self, you cannot offer good feelings to anyone else. Feeling good is not selfish, it is essential to living a good feeling life."

eleven

The crisp clear blue sky had changed during the four hours they had spent in the park. A wave of black clouds rolled towards the park obscuring the sun. These clouds seemed to hover so low that everyone could touch them. No one could touch the clouds, but the clouds reached down and anointed everyone.

The rain started with a few solitary large drops and then it pummelled the ground in sheets of water that sounded like a waterfall. People ran for cover from the surprise downpour. They ran under trees or hid under anything that deflected water. The rain was swift and stopped minutes after it had started. Many caught by the rain laughed with the other drenched people around them. A few danced in muddy puddles.

The clouds moved swiftly across the sky to the east after the storm. Their loss of moisture made them lighter in colour and weight. The wind split the clouds apart in shifting cracks and the sun streamed through in beams of light. These light ladders travelled from the clouds to the ground through the misty sky. In the mist, rainbow colours moved and shimmered in a dance. The drenched people looked into the sky filled with a joyful awe.

As the colours dazzled, the holes in the clouds increased and the shifting colours formed one glorious rainbow that arched its way across the sky.

"With practice you can see the light in everyone as you see those colours right now." Nicole said to Martin.

Martin Smiled

white

pier

Martin stood on the water's edge. Not on the mud and water border, but twenty feet above the ocean on a wooden pier. Seagulls soared in the wind beside Martin, moving up and down and from side to side but not forward or back. For an instant, Martin felt as if he were flying with them.

He turned his face into the wind and looked at the mountains in the distance. For a fraction of a second, Martin thought he saw the mountain's aura and all of its colours.

"With practice you can see the light in everyone as you see those colours right now." Martin said to himself.

"Did you see it?" Nicole appeared beside him.

"I think so."

"Wrong."

"What?"

"Not, I think. Choose to be that which you wish to see."

"Is it that simple?"

"Simple? Yes. Easy? No."

"How can I ever repay you?"

"Martin, with love you never have to repay you only have to give."

"Who do I give love to?"

"The question is not who do you give love to, but how much love do you give?"

"How much love do I give then?"

"Give as much as you can. First give love to yourself *selfishly* to build up your reserves and then give to as many people as you can, as often as you can. Even when you have next to nothing in material possessions, you always possess endless love that you have *selfishly* built up. It's that simple. We're all created equal; we're all made of pure love.

"This giving has a larger purpose too. Each of our souls is a part of a group of other souls. Only when all of the souls in our soul group move forward do we advance. That's not punishment. That's enlightenment!"

"Is that the reason loving our enemies is hard for us?"

"Our enemies are our best friends in spirit, and most are a part of our soul group. Together we plan little dramas for each other so that we can learn to love more. Our so-called enemies on earth present us with our greatest chances for advancement and we present theirs.

"Our actions even affect a soul group member who we have never met and will never meet in this lifetime, even when they live on the other side of the world. All of our actions affect others.

"That's kind of depressing."

"You mean impressing. The best thing about life is it is set up for everyone to win. We are always given everything we could ever need to accomplish our deepest heartfelt most secret dreams with God. All the time, energy, resources, and connections we need to accomplish our purpose in life are always present right now and we either see them as present now or we deny them.

"Be patient, persistent, and passionate about your dreams Martin and about the things you love. You rarely understand the purpose of the human experience while living it, but you shall understand the perfection of everything when you release your body and your limitations."

Martin and Nicole walked together from the beach and took the skytrain to the opposite end of town. They did not talk.

skytrain station

When they got off the skytrain, a couple approached Nicole to ask some questions. Nicole started talking and waved Martin off. Martin walked down the platform to give them more privacy. He stood in the sun and watched the people waiting for trains on the opposite platform. Martin tired to see their colourful auras. He could not see them, but he told himself that he would one day.

Nicole continued to talk and the couple slowly grew into a group of people. The sun moved across the sky and trains pulled regularly into and out of the station, going in both directions.

Down the platform, a man walked up to Martin and started

a conversation.

"That woman is so full of love." He said.

"Yes, she is." Martin agreed and smiled with the man.

"Gives you hope that this world has a positive future."

"Yes." Martin smiled.

Another train pulled into the station and the man Martin had been talking with got onto it. Martin smiled at the man after the train doors had shut and the train pulled away.

Chris rode the escalator up to the train platform situated six stories above the street. Halfway up the fifth story, the escalator stopped and Chris lunged forward hitting his knee.

"Crap!" he said.

Chris rubbed his knee and walked the final story up the halted escalator. At the top, Chris saw a group of people gathered around Nicole. He recognized her immediately and his temper began to boil hearing her words.

"We are all energy. We are all one loving oneness of energy here to bless each other through our actions." Nicole said.

"You people are brainwashed!" Chris yelled at everyone.

"Because we are happy?" Nicole said.

"Happy! You don't live in reality."

"You're right *Chris* - -"

Chris heard Nicole say his name and it registered for a millisecond, but his anger coursed through his veins and he had no control over himself.

Nicole continued, "- - we don't live in *your* reality."

"*Everybody's* reality!"

"Your *fear*, is not everyone's reality?"

"I'm not afraid!" he said.

"Only of what you don't understand."

"Oh! That we are all *energy*!" Chris mocked.

"Everything is energy."

"Your *lies* are energy?"

"We're all children of this energy and we create our reality with this God Life Energy."

"If I create my reality with this God Life Energy, then I'm divinely guided!"

"Everyone is divinely guided." Nicole said with a knowing smile.

Martin's eyes followed a train as it pulled out of the station past Nicole. The crowd around her had divided in half. For the first time Martin saw the back of a man at one end of the split and Nicole at the far end facing both Martin and the man screaming at her, "Go To Hell, Lady!"

Time slowed as Martin watched the man run up and shove Nicole towards the platform's railing. Martin screamed, "STOP!" Nicole smiled as she fell backwards and down out of sight over the railing.

The crowd stood absolutely stunned. Chris looked over the railing and then turned back to face the crowd. He lifted himself up until he sat on the railing and looked at each person in the crowd. Last he looked at Martin as he released his grip and leaned back. Chris smiled at Martin as he fell backwards and down out of sight.

Martin pushed himself through the crowd and looked over the edge. Both Nicole and Chris lay on the ground sixty feet below. Blood from their bodies stained the asphalt. The crowd quickly dispersed into their own individual worlds.

light

sensations

Chris felt strange and peaceful floating above his body. Actually he floated above two bodies, lying lifeless on the ground below him. He watched an ambulance arrive and paramedics survey the scene. Police kept people away, while the paramedics zipped the bodies into shiny black bags and placed them in the ambulance.

Chris followed the ambulance through the city. He knew his body was dead, but he did not know what else to do. In the hospital morgue he hung near the ceiling above the metal body cooler drawers.

light

The light that began to surround Chris was brighter than anything he could remember ever seeing. It was an iridescent light that was soothing to look at. He stared at the light as it crept into the hospital morgue. Every hue of colour he had never before imagined vibrated in its form. He did not fear it, yet he did not understand it either. The light was simultaneously flat and voluminous. The light created space and denied it. On the one hand it illuminated the space and surrounded Chris, on the other hand it created an impenetrable sphere into which he was denied access.

Chris then lost all sense of the hospital morgue. It was replaced by the perception of a definite infinite space. A loving space that enveloped him and made him feel at home. Earth had been a place where he had learned much, but the details were disappearing. This new infinite and defined space was more like his true home, more than earth had ever been. It connected to the centre of his being.

"Yes, that feeling is normal." the answer came to him in a voice that boomed louder than an explosion as it whispered into his soul.

"What is that feeling?" he asked in the same voice which was not vocal, but pure energy.

"Love."

"What happened to me?"

"Oneness was preparing to discuss that. What does Oneness remember?"

"I remember floating to the hospital." Chris said, but he could not remember anything else and he was forgetting even more. He looked at himself, he did not really have a form, but he glowed.

"Is this heaven?" Chris asked.

"Oneness could call it that."

"If this is heaven, was I good in my life?"

"Who is Oneness?"

"My name is . . . uh. . . are all of those my names?"

58

"Oneness has many names and is many things."

"I am . . . I am . . . I am everything?"

With that realization came awareness. Chris could no longer see his individuality; he could only see Oneness. He could not remember his names; he could only remember his namelessness. He could not remember himself; he could only remember Oneness.

"Remember." the Voiceless Voice said.

Images from the birth of Chris to the death of Chris flowed forth. Every thought, feeling, word, and action that Oneness had used during Chris' life were experienced again. Oneness experienced the use of energy and its effects on all things from Chris' viewpoint.

The sensations were more vibrant than Oneness remembered experiencing as Chris. The sensory information was powerful, but the energy fields around everything were even more amazing. These energy fields connected everything. Everything in life was connected by this iridescent light: every person with every animal with every tree with every plant with every rock with every seemingly lifeless part of the universe were all connected by vibrant sentient light.

When Oneness' recollection was complete, Oneness experienced the entire use of energy for a second time. This time Oneness experienced it from the receiving end of the energy used by Chris. Oneness felt how every thought, feeling, word, and action Chris had ever used affected everyone that came in contact with that energy. Oneness saw life with new understanding.

The Voiceless Voice communicated again, "What was the reason for this life as Chris?"

Oneness responded, "To give and receive love."

time

funeral

Martin could not forgive himself. His anger surfaced when he least wanted it. It also disappeared for long periods of time, only to turn up when he did not expect it. The funeral was one of those times.

Martin was angry with himself. If he had been closer to Nicole perhaps he could have saved her. Why did she not disappear before hitting the ground? He wished he had not listened to her request for privacy on the platform that day. He knew that was silly, he respected Nicole's opinion, yet he wondered how this experience helped him especially if on some level they had planned it together.

Martin was angry with Nicole. He blamed her because this cleverly disguised gift of love was too hard to understand. He did not know how to overcome his feelings of weakness. If he could not help Nicole, how could he help anyone? Even her final words for him at the pier did not curb his anger. ". . . you shall understand the perfection of everything when you release your body and your limitations."

Martin was angry with Chris. A few weeks earlier, Martin had hit Chris with his car. Nicole had saved Chris and then he rewarded Nicole with her own death. If Chris were not the perfect candidate for loving Nicole, who would be? How could anyone love their neighbour? How could anyone love their enemy?

Sitting in the funeral chapel, Martin realized that his anger was not helping him to control energy. Martin sat by himself and the funeral director left Martin alone to collect his thoughts.

Martin knew he could take all the time he wanted to understand this cleverly disguised gift of love. He could take days if he wanted. He could take years if he needed to. However he wondered what purpose that would serve. He had gained so much knowledge and he knew that he could share it. If he let his anger rule him, as it ruled him now, it would only attract more of the same feeling experiences to him.

But this burden was far too much for Martin. His heart ached with more pain than he thought he could ever know.

Nicole's words came to him again, "Let your pain go to let your joy grow. Just one thought that moves you to feel a little better is the way back to joy and if life ever seems too tough, let go of your painful burdens, and let God take care of them for you."

Martin sat there with his heart breaking and said a silent prayer. *Dear God, please take this burden from me. It is too big for me to bear alone.* And with this thought the vice grip around Martin's heart released and his fears faded and a lightness filled him with peace as he felt Nicole's loving presence beside him.

park

A month later Martin was walking through the park when he saw the back of a familiar form sitting on a bench.

"Nicole!" he screamed as he ran up to her side.

"Hello." a woman said, "I think you have mistaken me for

someone — ."

"I'm sorry." Martin said lost in his thoughts.

"Can I help you?"

He did not know what to say, then he said, "My name is Martin."

"My name is Claire." she said, "Won't you sit down, Martin."

The two talked together for hours with an ease you find in a soul family member whom has as many cleverly disguised gifts of love to share with you as you do with them.

a day to remember

A year had past since Nicole's transition. Claire and Martin stood together in front of family and friends and professed their undying love to each other.

"I wish to present; Mrs. Claire Sauvage and Mr. Martin Muller." the minister said.

The crowd stood and clapped and cheered and wished them all the best through their thoughts, feelings, words, and actions.

a night to remember

Six months later Claire made reservations at their favourite restaurant. At eight o'clock they arrived by taxi and were greeted by the owner.

"Claire, Martin," he said "It's good to see you both. I trust all is well?"

"Better than well." Claire said.

"Yes, better." Martin agreed.

"Married life seems to suit you both."

"We think so." they said in unison.

The owner escorted them to a table in a quite corner of the restaurant. Candles provided an opulent light.

"Would you like anything to drink this evening?" their waiter asked.

"Can you please bring us a pitcher of ice water, Please." Claire said.

"And the wine list?" Martin said.

The waiter handed the wine list to Martin, "I'll be back in a minute with your water."

Martin looked through the list and noticed a few wines he felt Claire would like.

"Which would you rather a white or a rose?"

"I'm not feeling very much like wine this evening."

"I thought we were celebrating six months tonight?"

"Sort of."

"Sort of?"

The waiter placed a cold and condensing pitcher of water on the table.

"Thank you." Claire said.

The waiter spoke, "Have you decided on a wine for this evening?"

"Not yet. Can you give us a few minutes, please?" Martin said.

"But of course." The waiter said and moved on to the next table.

"What do you mean . . . sort of?" Martin asked.

"Remember when we were talking the other night and you said that life is full of energy experiences."

"Sure."

"Well our latest use of energy has come back to us."

"It has?"

"Yes."

"You mean?"

"Yes." Claire said with a huge smile. "We're pregnant?"

Martin promenaded around the table to Claire. He picked

Claire up, kissed her, and then swung her around. "I love you! I love you both!" Martin yelled to everyone present, "I'm going to be a father."

Joyful applause greeted the three of them.

space

reunion

Oneness re-experienced the emotions of joy and pain from all sides of Chris' energy use. The energy had been both positive and negative. Positive for some people and negative for others with one notable exception.

"Hello." the exception spoke to him.

"Hello." Oneness responded.

"We planned this."

The images of this exception flowed through Oneness again. Rage was present in the energy of Chris, a powerful force with seemingly negative intentions. Love was present in the energy of Nicole, the most powerful of forces with infinite possibilities. The images then changed to a meeting before that particular lifetime. The energy frequencies of Chris and Nicole were joined in Oneness by Martin in that meeting.

"Life is fun, isn't it?" Nicole asked.

"Yes. So what now?" Oneness asked.

"Well Oneness can stay here Connected with All That Is and learn more or Oneness can go back and share this Loving

Oneness on Earth."

"Oneness would love to share love again."

"Remember, do what you really love. There are no mistakes."

the plan

The spirits of Claire, Martin, Chris, and Nicole gathered to plan a most delicious life journey towards love and joy together. Thousands of souls contributed to the plan. Souls of higher frequencies advised and guided the plan. The plan was inscribed with gold light onto a parchment like paper made of iridescent light.

The plan contained moments of total disconnection and despair. Incidents of ecstatic pleasure and passion were also written into the plan. Experiences of doubt and pain were arranged. The fulfilment of love and support were assured. Everything in the plan would be accomplished for the good of All That Is, no matter what appeared to be.

Most important in the plan was free will. This most random of factors in the design of life wherein Oneness could change the plan at anytime for the fun of it.

love

energy

Oneness floated in the living room above Martin and Claire and when it was time to change form, Oneness spoke with a voiceless voice that touched all of creation, "Thank you."

the big day

Two years to the day that Nicole died, Claire's water broke. Martin panicked a little as he drove to the hospital.

"Breathe deep." he said to calm himself more than Claire.

"I'm fine Martin." Claire said, "Ahhh!" she exhaled deeply.

"Are you alright?"

"Yeah . . . I'm . . . fine." she breathed and answered alternately.

They drove in record time to the hospital. A nurse used a

wheelchair to take Claire into a hospital room. Claire dressed in a crisp hospital gown and lay down on the bed. Claire was tranquil between contractions, but breathed heavily during them. When the time of birth approached Martin held Claire's hand and they breathed in synch.

"I love you." he said.

"I know."

Within minutes their doctor arrived and he told them that everything looked fine, "We're waiting for the little ones now."

"Ones?" Martin said.

Claire laughed, "You did know I was this big because of twins."

"I do now."

birth

"One more push, Claire." the doctor said.

"I can't." her voice strained.

"One more big breath beautiful." Martin encouraged her.

Together they sucked in air and together they exhaled. Claire groaned and the first baby gently slid free.

●●●

In that instant, Oneness could not see clearly and needed something desperately. Oneness took a huge breath of air and moaned softly.

●●●

"Congratulations!" the doctor said, "You have two beautiful baby girls."

The attending nurse gently wiped down the newborn babies and placed them onto Claire's chest. Their small loving forms suckled Claire's nipples.

Martin let go of everything that had been troubling him. He looked at his wife and baby girls. Around them a luminescence shimmered.

"Look at them, Claire." Martin cried excitedly, "They're beautiful like their mom!"

Tears ran down their faces. They had decided on some names before the birth, but in that moment different names came to mind and Claire said, "Let's call them Nicki and Chris."

"Let's."

They kissed and stared at Nicki and Chris and things continued as they always have. Loving Oneness expressing Loving Oneness with Loving Oneness eternally.

THE END

TO THE READER

For many years, I have been sharing my journey into increased Awareness and Oneness with God/Life/Energy with the people around me.

My work has primarily taken the form of non-fiction affirmative texts through my *I AM Creating My Own Experience* series of books.

When I speak to people about my journey, I share stories. Stories I have read, stories I have experienced, and stories I have written, some of which are yet to be released.

Many years ago, I wondered what it would be like to have a female messiah come into my life. It started as a short screenplay I wrote entitled *Seven Colours*. Then, I decided to work it into a feature length screenplay, yet I did not know the craft of screenplay writing well enough to flesh out the screenplay.

I next wrote it pretty much in its present structure and presented it to my writer's group where it was thoroughly described as too preachy. It was of course my first written baby and I did not want to throw it away. At the time, I had no clue how to move forward with it after it was so thoroughly agreed that I should let it go.

I did let it go and I let God do what God does. In the past fifteen years, I have worked on the craft of writing primarily as a journey of self-discovery, and secondarily to share my vision of hope with a world that at times appears to be lost.

The father of this story has been my appreciation of Richard Bach's *Illusions*. The mother of this story has been my appreciation of Esther and Jerry Hicks *Sara* Books.

Recently the idea of sharing some of my Inspirational fiction has come to the forefront again. Every time I began working on a story, *Loving Oneness* was in the back of my mind. God kept saying, "You can share it, for the fun of it." I have decided to do that. Here is *Loving Oneness* for the fun of it.

Enjoy Loving Oneness
Barry Thomas Bechta

ACKNOWLEDGEMENTS

I AM Eternally Grateful for God's Presence in my life. My Conscious Unification with each individualisation of God continually transforms my life in extraordinary ways. My world is Now GOD, Greatness Oneness Demonstrated.

I AM extremely grateful to Kimiko Nicole von Boetticher whom is the inspiration for the *Nicole* character. We were married at the time of this story's first incarnation in 1994.

I AM grateful to Binah C Godisall for the mirror she is in my life. I wish for her exactly what she wishes for herself as we experience the freedom of Unconditional Love together.

My child like gratitude bubbles forth to Anthony and Zachary. They both have reminded me that it is all just a fun game we are playing together.

Loving thanks to Stephen, Margaret, Gabe, and Sam for all their support as we continue to share our experience.

Warm thanks to my family by blood and by love. My Loving family grows in Oneness each day.

I AM grateful to all the authors that continually inspire me to challenge and expand any limits in my view of God, Love, and Life.

Once again thank you to everyone who has ever helped me in any way over the years.

I love all of you very much

ABOUT THE AUTHOR

Barry Thomas Bechta is an artist, author, and film maker whose work centers around the concepts of Unconditional Love. Barry knew he wanted to write from a very young age and was encouraged with his artistic skills and only began writing full time in his thirties. He wrote his first book, *I AM Creating My Own Experience* as a personal journal to choose connection with God/Life/Energy. He has since written 17 inspirational spiritual books.

Barry loves to hear from people whom have connected with his writing and used it as a tool to improve their lives. If you would like to write him about your personal experiences as a result of reading any of his books, Barry encourages you to do so.

You can also get a Free Digital Copy of *I AM Creating My Own Experience - The Creation Vibration* from his main website:

www.unconditionallovebooks.com

Unconditional Love Books Titles of Related Interest by Barry Thomas Bechta

I AM Creating My Own Experience
978-0-9813485-5-1

I AM Creating My Own Answers
978-0-9686835-1-4

I AM Creating My Own Dreams
978-0-9686835-2-1

I AM Creating My Own Relationships
978-0-9686835-3-8

I AM Creating My Own Abundance
978-0-9686835-4-5

I AM Creating My Own Success
978-0-9686835-5-2

I AM Creating My Own Happiness
978-0-9686835-6-9

I AM Creating My Own Experience - The Creation Vibration
978-0-9686835-7-6

I AM Creating My Own Experience - To Manifest Money
978-0-9686835-8-3

I AM Creating My Own Experience - 369 Conscious Days
978-0-9686835-9-0

Loving Oneness
978-0-9813485-0-6

Trust Life
978-0-9813485-1-3

I AM Creating My Own Financial Freedom - The Story
978-0-9813485-2-0

I AM Creating My Own Financial Freedom - The Lessons
978-0-9813485-3-7

Laughing Star's Guide to Laughter, Life, Love, and God
978-0-9813485-4-4

All of the above are books are available through your local bookstore, or they may be ordered as digital downloads at
www.unconditionallovebooks.com

Barry Thomas Bechta is available for interviews, special events, workshops, and lectures that redefine, guide, and inspire everyone's connection to the Creative Power within themselves. To arrange author interviews, special events, workshops, or lectures, please contact:

UNCONDITIONAL LOVE BOOKS

Unconditional Love Books
Box # 610 - 2527 Pine St.,
Vancouver, BC, Canada V6J 3E8

info@unconditionallovebooks.com

www.unconditionallovebooks.com

For additional copies of Barry's books, products, and services please contact your local book seller. Many products and services are Only available to order directly from the publisher as eProducts on the website.

Thanks for your purchase and Remember to Consciously Create your Life.

Right Now is the Only Moment of Creation

Enjoy it Fully!